DI

D0504414

NORMAN
PRICE

BELLA
LASAGNE

JAMES

SARAH

TITLES AVAILABLE IN BUZZ BOOKS

First published 1990 by Buzz Books,
an imprint of the Octopus Publishing Group,
Michelin House, 81 Fulham Road, London, SW3 6RB.

LONDON MELBOURNE AUCKLAND

Fireman Sam © 1985 Prism Art & Design Ltd

Text © 1990 William Heinemann Ltd

Illustrations © 1990 William Heinemann Ltd
Story by Caroline Hill-Trevor
Illustrations by CLIC
Based on the animation series produced by Bumper Films for
S4C/Channel 4 Wales and Prism Art & Design Ltd.
Original idea by Dave Gingell and Dave Jones, assisted by
Mike Young. Characters created by Rob Lee.

ISBN 1 85591 010 1

Printed and bound in the UK by BPCC Paulton Books Ltd.

A BAD DAY FOR DILYS

Story by Caroline Hill-Trevor
Illustrations by CLIC!

buzz books

"That's it for today then, Fireman Sam. It's early closing," said Dilys, as she closed her shop.

"Enjoy your half-day, Dilys. Put your feet up for a change!" smiled Fireman Sam, as he left the shop. "I wish I could have the afternoon off but I'm on standby today."

"At last," sighed Dilys. "What a morning! The whole village seems to have been in, not that I'm complaining, of course."

Dilys walked slowly upstairs. "I suppose I'd better have a go at that pile of washing or Norman will need some new clothes!"

"How did we manage before there were washing machines?" she murmured, as she gathered up all Norman's sports gear. "I'll just set this lot going and then I'll treat myself to a cup of tea and a biscuit."

8

Dilys poured herself a cup of tea and then sat down and closed her eyes. "I'll fetch that biscuit," she remembered a moment later, and jumped up.

"Aagh! My feet are soaking!"

There was a big puddle of soapy water spreading across the kitchen floor. "Oh no, the machine's leaking," said Dilys, as she splashed about. "Never mind. I'll just have to wash the clothes by hand."

"These clothes will dry in no time," Dilys thought, as she went outside. "Yes, no time at all," she said, hanging onto the clothes as they caught the wind. But the wind was strong and, as she pegged up the last shirt, an enormous gust swept through the garden, taking the washing line with it.

All Dilys's clean washing was blowing around the garden. "Help! Help!" she cried as she chased after it.

"These clothes are covered in mud," grumbled Dilys. "I suppose I'll have to wash them all over again now."

12

"That's funny," Dilys thought. "I'm sure Norman's spare rugby shirt was in this pile somewhere. It's not my day today. Never mind, I can put everything in the tumble dryer. Where would I be without it?"

13

But she spoke too soon. As she sat down the
tumble dryer stuttered and spluttered and
then stopped altogether. Dilys tried the
switch again, but it was no good, the dryer
wouldn't work. "This is too much," she
wailed, "all this modern equipment and
none of it works. Now what am I going to do?"

"I'll just have to hang them up inside. At
least I can start on the ironing – Norman
needs a rugby shirt for the match tomorrow."

With her fingers crossed, Dilys got out the iron. It seemed to be working fine. Carefully, she set to work on the pile of damp clothes.

"I do enjoy ironing," hummed Dilys, as she looked at the neatly-pressed shirts and the shrinking pile of clothes beside her. "So satisfying, it always cheers me up."

17

The 'phone rang. "I hope that's the electrician calling back," thought Dilys. "Oh, hello, Bella. You've found Norman's spare shirt? Must have been blown out of the garden."

18

As Dilys chatted away she forgot that she'd left the iron down. Soon there was a suspicious burning smell coming from the ironing board.

19

"Hello, Mum," said Norman, coming
through the door. "Been doing some
cooking, have you?" he asked, looking
around. Then he saw smoke coming from
the ironing board. "Oh no, fire! Fire!" he
shouted. "Come on, Mum, get outside. The
ironing board's on fire."

20

Dilys quickly unplugged the iron and
they both went outside. They ran across the
road to Bella's Café.

"Quick, Bella, call the Fire Brigade.
There's a fire in my house," cried Dilys.

"Dial 999, quick," yelled Norman.

21

Up at the fire station, Fireman Sam and
Fireman Elvis Cridlington were on standby
when the message came through on the
automatic printer.

"Ironing board fire at Dilys Price's," read
Elvis Cridlington.

22

"Quick, ring the alarm. Irons can start serious fires; the whole house could go up in flames," said Fireman Sam.

They jumped into Jupiter and set off through the village with the siren wailing and the lights flashing.

Jupiter drew up outside the shop.
"Where's the fire, Dilys?" asked Fireman
Sam, looking at the smoke.

"The ironing board, in the kitchen," Dilys
wailed. "Hurry, please."

24

"Don't worry, Dilys," said Elvis,
"Fireman Sam's the man for the job."

Fireman Sam put on his mask and went
inside. Using a fire extinguisher, he quickly
put out the flames.

"Panic over, Dilys," he said, when he
came out again. "You were very lucky;
there's not much damage but I'm afraid
you'll have to wash all those clothes again.
The smoke has made them very dirty."

26

Dilys sighed. "I've already washed
everything twice. Still, if you hadn't come
to the rescue, I wouldn't have any clothes
to wash! Thank you, Fireman Sam."

"Not much damage!" cried Norman. "My best rugby shirt is ruined. What am I going to wear for the match tomorrow?"

"Don't worry, my lovely," said Dilys. "Bella found your spare shirt. I'll wash it again. You can wear that for now."

"Thanks, Mum," laughed Norman, "but I think I'll wash it myself. It doesn't seem to be your day today, and I've only got one spare shirt!"

FIREMAN SAM

STATION OFFICER
STEELE

TREVOR EVANS

ELVIS
CRIDLINGTON